This edition published in Great Britain in MMXIX
by Scribblers, an imprint of
The Salariya Book Company Ltd
25 Marlborough Place,
Brighton BN1 1UB

© Mijade Publications MMXIII
Text © Jessica Martinello MMXIII
Illustrations © Grégoire Mabire MMXIII
English translation by Jane Singleton Paul
English language © The Salariya Book Company Ltd MMXIX

HB ISBN-13: 978-1-912537-75-4

1 3 5 7 9 8 6 4 2

A CIP catalogue record for this book is
available from the British Library.

Printed and bound in Belgium

Printed on paper from sustainable sources

Visit
www.salariya.com
for our online catalogue and
free fun stuff.

For my mum and dad, for all their support and all they taught me...
and for making me brush my teeth every night when I was a child.
Oh! And for my friend, the Hairy Monster!

J.M.

For Saadet

G.M.

TOOTH MONSTERS

Written by
Jessica Martinello

Illustrated by
Grégoire Mabire

S

SCRIBBLERS

a SALARIYA imprint

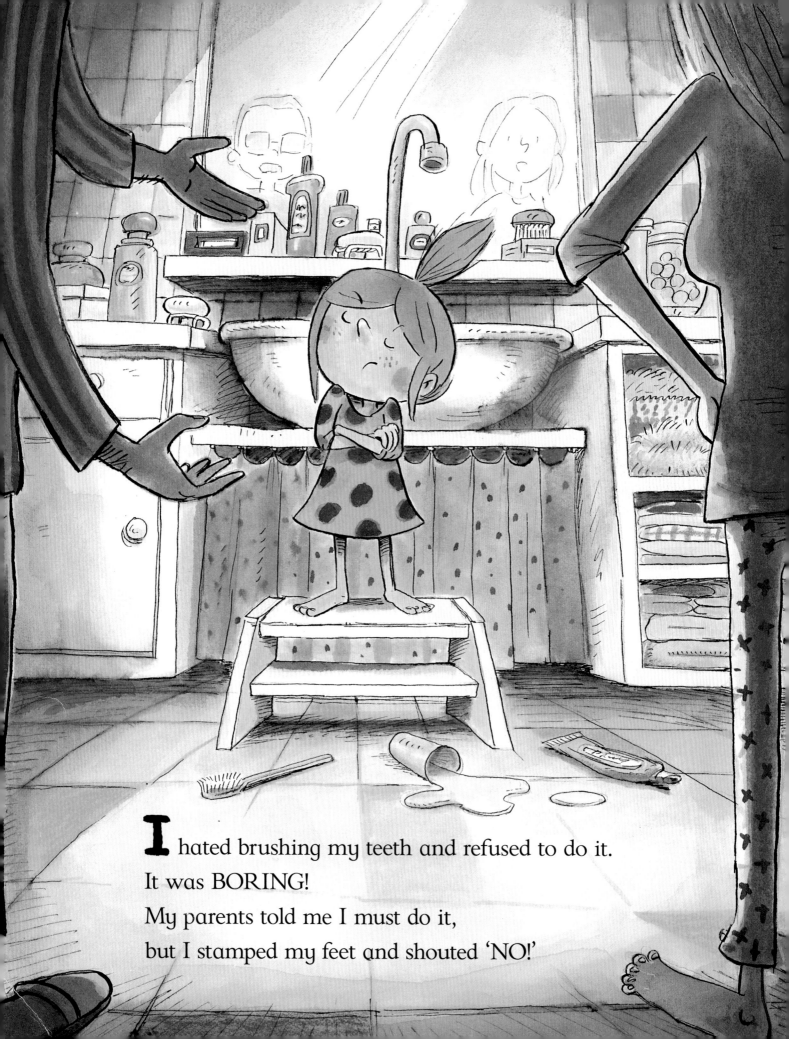

I hated brushing my teeth and refused to do it.
It was BORING!
My parents told me I must do it,
but I stamped my feet and shouted 'NO!'

Have you ever met a monster?
For me, the scariest monster of all was the dentist!
I was terrified of the dentist until...

...One night, I was in the bathroom.

I was supposed to be brushing my teeth when, suddenly, the shower curtain beside me moved.

AAAAAAAAAAAAHHHHHHHHHHH!!!

A monster!

A huge, hairy monster was brushing his teeth in the shower!

I ran for my life but... nobody believed me. I was sent back to the bathroom to brush my teeth.

'You'll need a better excuse next time!' said Dad.

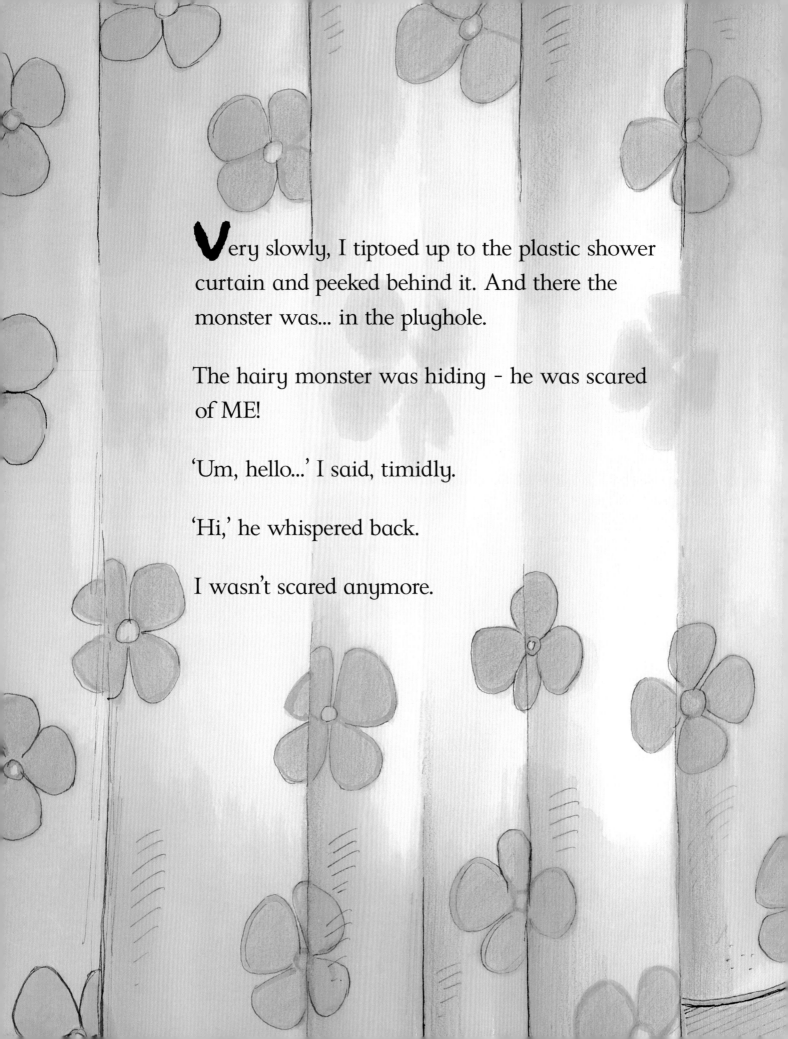

Very slowly, I tiptoed up to the plastic shower curtain and peeked behind it. And there the monster was... in the plughole.

The hairy monster was hiding - he was scared of ME!

'Um, hello...' I said, timidly.

'Hi,' he whispered back.

I wasn't scared anymore.

'**W**hy were you brushing your teeth?'
I asked him. 'I hate brushing mine.'

'But you MUST do it!' cried the
monster, looking worried. 'If you
don't, you'll be in big trouble!'

He climbed out of the shower
and sat beside me.

'All monsters, even the ugliest
ones, brush their teeth.
It's VERY important!'

'You know the monster under the bed?
Well, his gums are very delicate.
His toothbrush is made of children's
hair because it is so soft. That's why
he's always under the bed, collecting it.'

'And the Loch Ness monster - you must have heard of him?

Nessie brushes his teeth at least twice a day, and he has lots of teeth to clean!

A team of gnomes help him because food often gets stuck in places he can't reach.'

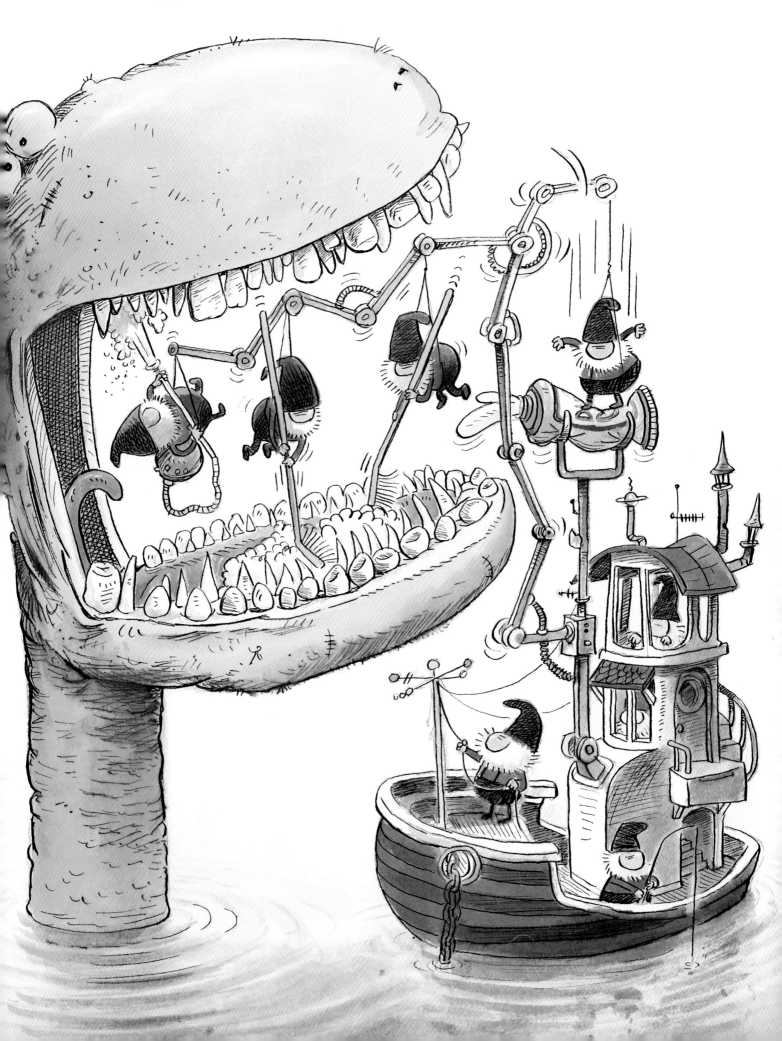

'**E**ven the basement monster brushes her teeth, well... tooth - she only has ONE!

But she brushes it morning and night for at least two minutes.

She's a very busy monster, with no free time, and still...'

'**B**ut the very worst monster ever... should be avoided at all costs,' the hairy monster whispered.

'WORST? I don't believe it. Worse than the dentist?' I asked.

'YES! Much, much worse. It's called...'

'Cavity Monster!

There are lots of them. They're small and friendly-looking, but they have hammers... and love attacking teeth: monsters' teeth, children's teeth, animals' teeth, in fact - ANY TEETH!'

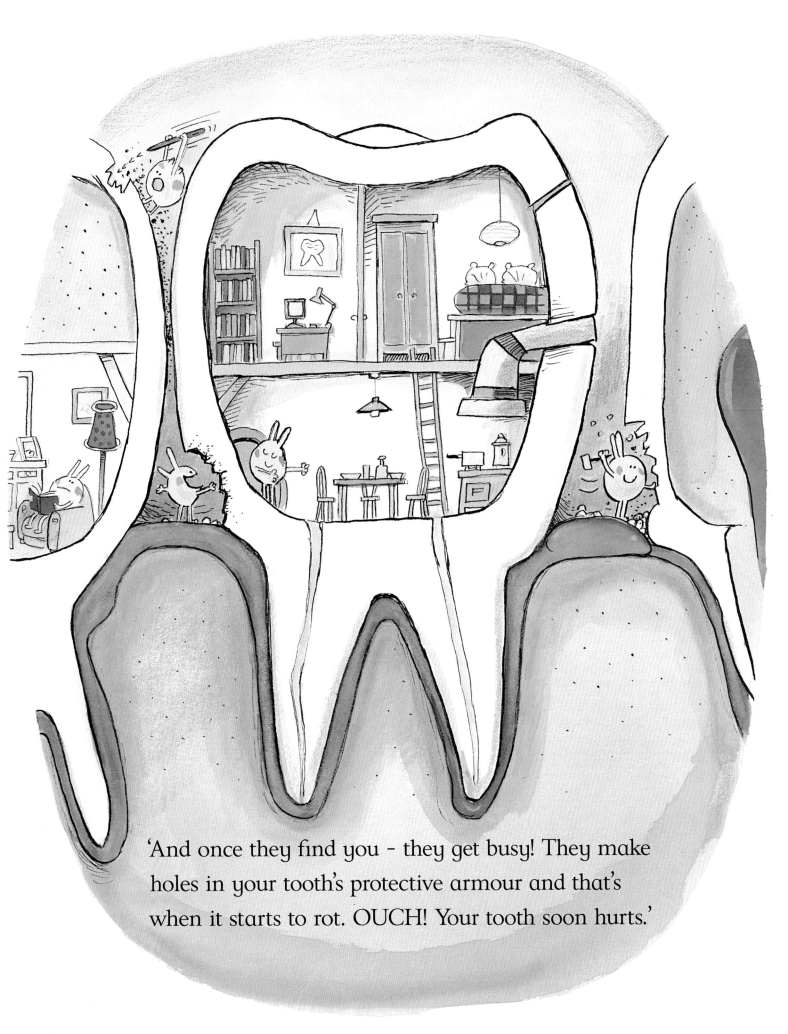

'And once they find you - they get busy! They make holes in your tooth's protective armour and that's when it starts to rot. OUCH! Your tooth soon hurts.'

'**B**ut a few simple tricks can beat the Cavity Monsters!
Brush your teeth morning and evening for at least
two minutes.

Don't forget toothpaste - it helps
to keep the monsters out.

Eat good food - plenty
of milk, cheese, fruit and
raw vegetables.

And try your very hardest... **NOT TO EAT SWEETS!'**

'And if that doesn't defeat the Cavity Monsters, there's always someone who can... the dentist.'

'NO! Not the dentist! The dentist is the real monster,' I cried.

'Not at all,' said the hairy monster, smiling. 'Your dentist is a superhero! Dentists come to the rescue and repair your teeth. They wear masks so the cavity monsters don't recognise them as they come to get them.'

'Okay, okay, I get it... but brushing your teeth is still really boring.'

'Well...' said the hairy, not-so-scary monster, 'it doesn't have to be. Try brushing beside someone else, or brush in the shower, like I do, or dance while you're brushing.

Then you'll never get bored brushing your teeth again!'